A MAGIC CIRCLE BOOK

THE BUMBERSHOOT

story by **BRUCE HAMMOND** and **LUCINDA WINSLOW**
pictures by **BRUCE HAMMOND**

THEODORE CLYMER
SENIOR AUTHOR, READING 360

GINN AND COMPANY
A XEROX EDUCATION COMPANY

IJ 08543210
PRINTED IN THE UNITED STATES OF AMERICA
0-663-30757-0